EXTREME CAREERS™

FIRST RESPONDERS

Allan B. Cobb

rosen publishing's
rosen
central®

New York

Published in 2007 by The Rosen Publishing Group, Inc.
29 East 21st Street, New York, NY 10010

First Edition

Library of Congress Cataloging-in-Publication Data

Cobb, Allan B.
First responders / Allan B. Cobb.
p. cm.—(Extreme careers)
Includes bibliographical references and index.
ISBN-13: 978-1-4042-0944-2
ISBN-10: 1-4042-0944-1 (library binding)
1. Emergency medical technicians—Juvenile literature. 2. Emergency medical services—Juvenile literature. I. Title. II. Series.
RA645.5.C53 2007
362.18—dc22

2006008491

Manufactured in the United States of America

On the cover: Coast Guard first responders rescue those trapped in New Orleans' floodwaters after Hurricane Katrina.

Contents

Introduction

Imagine this scenario. On a rainy night, a car is driving down a desolate road. A deer jumps in front of the car. The driver swerves and loses control of the car, and the car slides off the road and hits a tree. The airbag deploys and prevents serious injury. However, the driver has a broken arm from the accident.

A woman passing by sees the accident and quickly calls 911 on her cell phone. She gives the operator the location of the accident. The operator calls the first responders team, which may include the police, the fire department, and the emergency medical services (EMS) ambulance, among others. The ambulance crew of first responders, which consists of two emergency medical technicians, or EMTs, is jolted awake by the alarm. The EMTs scramble to their ambulance and head out to the accident.

When the EMTs arrive at the scene of the accident, the police may already be there. The accident victim, or patient, is still waiting in the car. The EMTs quickly grab their gear, go to the car, and check the patient. The equipment they carry allows them to perform some of the same procedures that would be done at a hospital. By having the equipment with them, they save valuable time in determining the condition of the patient.

If needed, the first responders can provide the patient with oxygen or use equipment to restart his heart, if necessary. The first responders are trained to perform these functions quickly and under stress. For some accident patients, this is the difference between life and death.

The first responders assess, or check out, the driver and find that his broken arm is the only injury. In this case, the accident patient's injuries are not critical. The first responders use a splint to immobilize his arm and load him onto a gurney. They wheel the patient to the ambulance and lift him gently into the back of the vehicle.

With the siren blaring, the ambulance drives off to the nearest hospital. One of the EMTs drives the ambulance while the other rides in the back with the

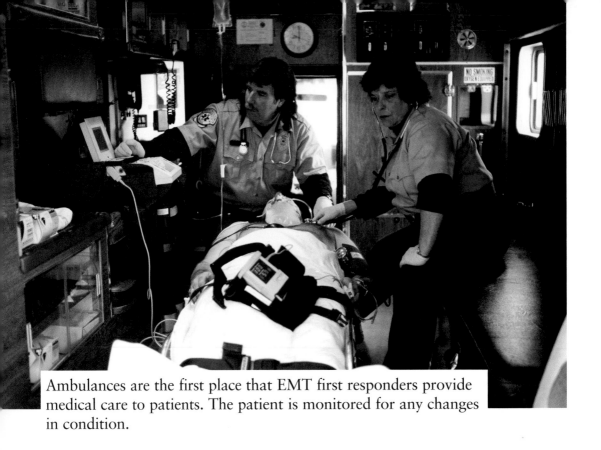

Ambulances are the first place that EMT first responders provide medical care to patients. The patient is monitored for any changes in condition.

accident patient. When they reach the hospital, they hand off the patient to the waiting doctors and nurses for further treatment. The EMTs then return to their posts and wait for the next call.

Being a first responder, such as these EMTs, is a physically demanding job. They spend considerable time kneeling, standing, and lifting heavy loads. They also have to work in all sorts of weather conditions. Calls come during storms and other natural disasters, as well as from different types of accidents. In addition, first responders often work long and irregular hours.

Not only is the job physically demanding, it may also be emotionally draining. First responders routinely work under high-stress conditions and make life-or-death decisions for their patients. Not all patients survive their injuries, and first responders must accept death as part of their job.

First responders also face other dangers on the job. Sometimes they must work under hazardous conditions to reach patients. Sometimes at accident scenes, secondary accidents occur when passing motorists are busy watching the accident instead of paying attention to driving. First responders may also be put into situations where they are shot at, or work alongside the fire department at a fire. They may be exposed to smoke or hazardous fumes from the fire, such as in hazardous chemical rescue.

These outside threats are not the only danger first responders face. The patients themselves may also pose a hazard. Some patients may have serious transmittable diseases such as AIDS or hepatitis. First responders do what they can to protect themselves from any contaminated body fluids by wearing protective equipment such

When Hurricane Katrina devastated New Orleans in 2005, first responders were called in from across the United States to assist.

as gloves and masks. Sometimes, first responders must deal with violent patients and risk being injured by them.

This is the type of work that is typically performed by first responders. These people dedicate their time to helping people in life-threatening situations. Sometimes the calls are rather minor. At other times, the actions of the first rescuers save the lives of the patients involved.

First Responder Training

1

The first people to respond to an emergency call are, as their title implies, the first responders. The first responders are rescue professionals—including police, firefighters, and other recovery experts—who have special training in emergency medicine. Though they may be known as first responders, they are certified and officially known as emergency medical technicians when involved in rescue situations. This is because first responders are required to have some degree of EMT training.

EMTs in Emergency Health Care

EMTs receive specialized training that they use when responding to emergencies. This includes a wide variety of medical procedures. They are trained to open airways to restore breathing, control blood loss, and treat shock. They also carry and are trained to use equipment and materials such as stretchers, backboards, oxygen, and defibrillators.

When EMTs respond to a call, they are prepared to do what is needed to stabilize a patient for transport. This might involve using cardiopulmonary resuscitation (CPR) on a patient whose heart has stopped. CPR is a technique that uses rescue breathing (mouth-to-mouth resuscitation) and chest compressions to maintain blood and oxygen flow in a patient. This procedure may cause the heart to start beating on its own, or it may give the EMTs time to use a defibrillator. EMTs might also use a defibrillator to shock a person's heart to cause it to start beating again. The EMTs might otherwise hook a patient up to an electrocardiogram (EKG) to monitor his or her heart rhythm and diagnose what type of heart problem he or she may have (an EKG is an instrument that makes an electrical recording of the heart).

The EMTs are in constant communication with doctors, who can direct them on what needs to be done with the patient. Some EMTs even have specialized and

Ambulances carry the life-saving equipment first responders need, such as EKGs, as well as radios to keep in constant contact with both the dispatcher and the hospital.

advanced training and are better able to assess and treat patients prior to transport to a hospital.

Emergency Medicine Training

All first responders are trained with basic medical knowledge needed to assess and stabilize a patient. They perform various medical procedures, but they usually do not administer any medications. Paramedics, however, receive advanced training in injury assessment and treatment. Considering this, they may give medicine and may provide medical support similar to a doctor. Both EMTs and paramedics are trained to stabilize patients and transport them to a hospital if needed. The first responders work as a team, each doing his or her job as quickly as possible.

When people think about first responders, they think about these basic duties. However, few people stop to think about how first responders are trained to do their job. Just like nurses and doctors, first responders go through a rigorous training program to learn their skills.

Each state and the District of Columbia require that first responders are certified as EMTs. Most states require registration with the National Registry of Emergency Medical Technicians (NREMT). The NREMT has a program that certifies EMTs at certain levels based on the skills they are trained to perform. Some states have their own programs to certify EMTs. The certification levels are similar to those established by the NREMT.

First responder training is demanding because of the amount of information that must be learned. First responders must be able to correctly perform their jobs under pressure. Many times, lives depend on the decisions and care given by the first responders.

The educational backgrounds of people who enter EMT programs vary widely. The minimum requirements for acceptance are a high school diploma or a General Educational Development (GED) certificate. The EMT training may be taken and used toward gaining an associate's degree. Some people enter the program with a college degree. Others enter the EMT program as a midlife career change and may come from just about any background.

EMTs and paramedics are required to be re-registered every two years. To meet the re-registration requirements,

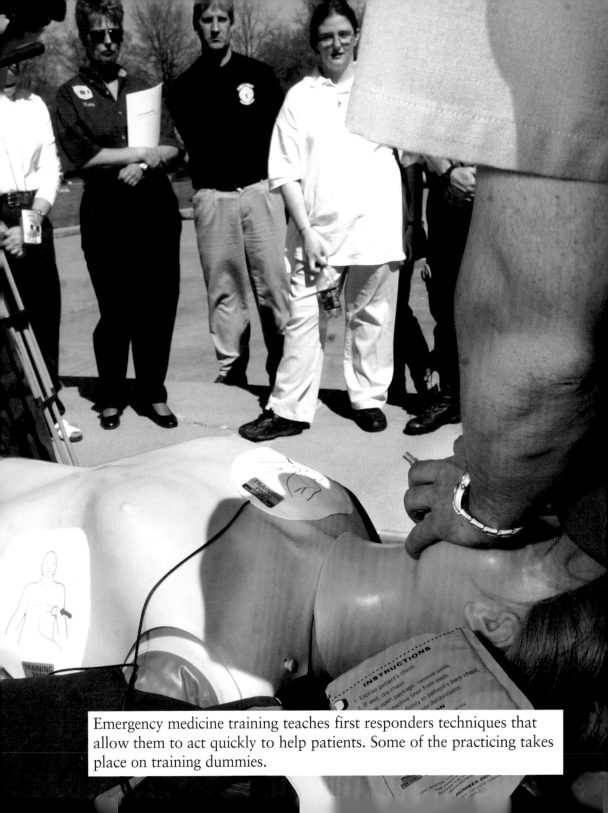

Emergency medicine training teaches first responders techniques that allow them to act quickly to help patients. Some of the practicing takes place on training dummies.

they must complete continuing education courses. In these courses, they learn new techniques and any other advances that have come about in emergency medicine.

EMT-Basic

EMT-Basic, sometimes called EMT-1, is a course that requires the least amount of training to become registered. In some states, this level of certification classifies a person as a first responder. An EMT-Basic goes through 100 to 120 hours of classroom training. In the classroom, the student learns basic medical terminology, anatomy, physiology, and patient assessment. The student also learns skills such as CPR, immobilization of fractures, controlling bleeding, and performing childbirth. Students also learn how to protect themselves from hazardous materials and diseases that can be transmitted through blood, like hepatitis and AIDS.

In addition to classroom training, a twenty- to fifty-hour internship in the field with a rescue unit or ambulance unit, and ten hours of hospital emergency room internship, are required. All the internship hours are performed under supervision from a paramedic. During the internship period, the student gains firsthand experience on how to perform the job. This experience includes administering physical exams on a patient, maintaining an open breathing airway, providing oxygen, and using a defibrillator. The student also learns to drive an emergency vehicle. After completing all these requirements, the trainee must pass both written and practical examinations. Once the examinations are passed, the title of Registered EMT-Basic is awarded.

EMT-Intermediate

EMT-Intermediate training varies from state to state. Some states break down EMT-Intermediate into EMT-2 and EMT-3. In other states, it is broken down into EMT-Shock Trauma and EMT-Cardiac. Entry into an EMT-Intermediate training program requires an EMT-Basic certification and an additional thirty-five to fifty-five hours of instruction and field training. The additional training provides the EMT with more in-depth knowledge in the areas of patient assessment, intravenous (IV) fluids, basic medications, and esophageal airways.

In the states with EMT-Shock Trauma and EMT-Cardiac certification, the EMT gets specialized training in one of those areas. The EMT-Shock Trauma coursework

Education is ongoing for first responders. They receive additional specialized training to be certified to perform any number of specific procedures.

teaches the EMT to start IV fluids and give certain medications to prevent or treat shock in badly injured patients. The EMT-Cardiac coursework teaches the EMT how to interpret heart rhythms and administer advanced medicines.

As in any job, EMTs who take the additional training for the EMT-Intermediate level are given more responsibility on the job, and pay raises come with the increased responsibility. EMT-Intermediate training is also usually required to advance to the highest EMT level, the paramedic.

EMT-Paramedic

The highest level of EMT is the paramedic. To become an EMT-Paramedic, or EMT-4 in some states, a student must already have an EMT-Basic or, in some states, an EMT-Intermediate certification. The EMT-Paramedic program usually results in a two-year associate's degree. The program requires 750 to 2,000 hours of extensive coursework, field training, and hospital work experience. Students review all previous training, as well as receive advanced training in other lifesaving skills.

An EMT-Paramedic is trained to interpret EKG results, treat collapsed lungs, and administer various methods for reestablishing breathing in patients. EMT-Paramedics are also trained to use medications to treat cardiac arrest, diabetic reactions, allergic reactions, and respiratory complications.

EMTs and paramedics are responsible for emergency medical care of persons involved in any number of incidents. These include violent assaults, strokes, and serious accidents. As first responders, they offer this

To become an EMT, it's important to receive as much education in the sciences and medicine as possible. This education can begin as early as high school.

care by responding to calls swiftly and reacting to the situation based on their training.

How to Become an EMT

Most states require a minimum of a high school diploma or GED to enter an EMT program. The person must also be in good physical shape because he or she must carry heavy equipment and possibly patients. As with any profession, the more education a person has, the easier it may be to find future advancement. These steps provide basic information that is helpful for someone who wants to become an EMT:

1. Take as many high school courses as possible in biology, chemistry, and health, along with driver's education.

2. Volunteer with your local ambulance or rescue squad. This can provide valuable real-life EMT experience.

3. Enroll in a basic EMT training program offered by the municipal police, fire department, health department, or community college for certification.

To become an EMT, it's important to begin your education as early as possible. If you have an interest in becoming an EMT, take as many appropriate classes as you can and enroll in extracurricular activities that provide you with experience for the job.

Responding to the Call

2

If an accident or injury occurs, the first thing people usually do is call 911. When someone calls 911, an operator records the information from the call. The operator takes down all the important details, such as the location of an accident and the nature of any injuries. The operator then transfers the call to the appropriate first responder department.

Emergency Medical Technicians

If the emergency is medical, such as a car accident, the dispatcher contacts the closest EMS unit and gives the information to the EMTs. The EMTs jump into their ambulance, turn on the siren, and head for the scene of the accident or location of the injury. EMTs usually work

First responders sometimes trade their ambulances for helicopters. They may fly to remote locations where ambulance access isn't possible to pick up victims and transport them to a hospital.

in teams. Each ambulance typically carries two first responders.

When the EMTs arrive on the scene, their actions are coordinated with the dispatcher and, if needed, with doctors at a hospital. Upon arriving, the first job of the EMTs is to assess the injuries of the patient or patients and take their medical history. Then the EMTs can provide medical care. In some cases, this means transporting patients to a hospital. In other cases, they must act quickly to stop bleeding, restore breathing, or even restart a patient's heart. Since paramedics have considerably more training than regular EMTs, they may be able to perform treatments on patients so that the patients do not need to be transported to a hospital— the advanced training can actually replace a hospital visit in some cases. Sometimes, the paramedic consults with doctors over the radio before performing any medical procedures.

If the patient has a back or neck injury, a backboard or cervical collar is used for support and protection. The patient is then loaded into an ambulance. During the ride to the hospital, the patient's condition is monitored by one of the EMTs while the other drives. In some cases, additional procedures may be performed in the ambulance while en route to the hospital.

Sometimes, a patient's condition is too critical for a long ride to the hospital. Many EMS services in large cities use specially equipped helicopters to transport patients to a hospital. As with an ambulance, the helicopter has an EMT who monitors the patient. The helicopter is also stocked with any lifesaving equipment that might be needed while in flight. In addition, helicopters have the advantage of being able to travel faster and avoid traffic. This gets the patient to the hospital and into an emergency room more quickly and efficiently.

Upon arrival at the hospital, the EMTs help take the patient out of the ambulance and transport him or her into the hospital. The EMTs tell the hospital's emergency medical personnel what care they have provided, any information regarding the patient's condition, and details of the patient's injuries. At this point, the emergency staff at the hospital takes over and continues caring for the patient.

After delivering the patient to the hospital, the EMTs prepare their vehicle for the next call by replenishing

When police and firefighters are the first responders at the scene of an accident, they provide immediate care for the patient and stabilize him or her until the ambulance arrives.

their supplies and cleaning the interior of the ambulance. If they have transported a patient with some kind of contagious disease, they may need to decontaminate the interior and possibly the exterior of the ambulance.

Police and Firefighters

Many emergency professionals, like police and firefighters, provide some level of medical care because they are usually the first people to arrive at an accident or fire scene. When a police officer arrives at the scene of an accident, it may still be several minutes before an ambulance is able to get there. In rural areas, the police officer may arrive at the scene long before the ambulance does. A police officer carries medical equipment in his or her car and can start treatment before the ambulance arrives. This saves critical time and may save lives.

Many fire departments also have their firefighters trained to at least the first responder or EMT-1 level. This is very helpful during large-scale accidents or disasters, when firefighters can then switch their role to helping the sick or injured. This has been particularly helpful after tornadoes, floods, and hurricanes.

Law Enforcement Tactical Teams

Many police forces have tactical teams. These specialized teams go after dangerous criminals in an organized way so that the threat to the officers' safety is minimized. The EMT-Tactical (EMT-T) team is a vital part of the police force. The EMT-T not only has all the specialized weapons and tactical training as the other officers on

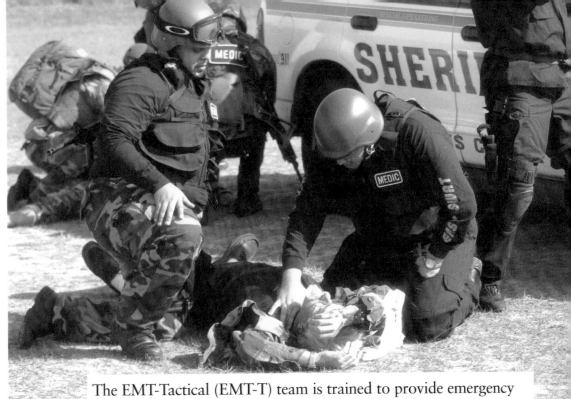

The EMT-Tactical (EMT-T) team is trained to provide emergency care in high-risk situations, like police raids. EMT-Ts are critical due to the extreme danger involved in their line of work.

the team, but he or she also has special medical training to deal with the types of injuries that may need to be treated. This line of work is very dangerous because of the violent nature of the criminals they target. However, the EMT-T often spends more time maintaining equipment and in training than actually using his or her first responder skills.

EMT-Ts are often part of special weapons and tactics (SWAT) police teams. EMT-Ts have specialized training

Not only do EMT-Ts treat injured law enforcement professionals, like SWAT teams, they also help anyone who may be harmed in a law-enforcement conflict.

in dealing with gunshot wounds and other types of injuries that may happen to members of the SWAT team, the people they are after, or bystanders.

Often, when a SWAT team member is injured, it is too dangerous to bring in EMTs to prepare the patient for transport to the hospital. The EMT-T must keep the patient stabilized until it is OK to move him or her to a safe facility. Since EMT-Ts work outside of medical facilities, they face many problems regarding working in difficult environments. They often have to work with minimal equipment and may be isolated from outside medical help.

Rescue Operations

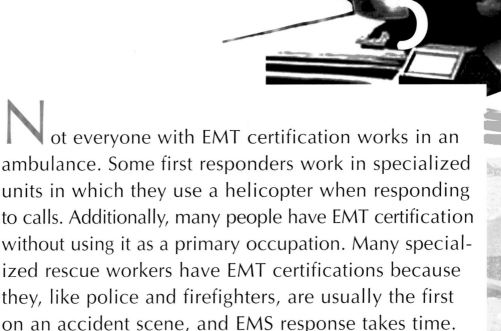

Not everyone with EMT certification works in an ambulance. Some first responders work in specialized units in which they use a helicopter when responding to calls. Additionally, many people have EMT certification without using it as a primary occupation. Many specialized rescue workers have EMT certifications because they, like police and firefighters, are usually the first on an accident scene, and EMS response takes time. These rescue workers use their skills to stabilize patients until other help arrives, such as in a search and rescue team.

Search and Rescue

Search and rescue (SAR) personnel can be either volunteers or full-time professionals. Many SAR personnel also have EMT certification. When SAR personnel are called upon to rescue someone, they often go to remote locations. They may be looking for lost hikers, people trapped by avalanches, or people lost at sea. SAR personnel train for each specific type of rescue in which they may be involved.

One of the most common types of SAR work is finding lost people. Each year, thousands of people become lost while hiking, camping, skiing, or performing other outdoor activities. SAR personnel go out and find them. Often, SAR experts cover large areas of remote land by foot, horseback, all-terrain vehicle, jeep, or helicopter. When they find the lost person or group, they provide medical treatment when necessary. Because of the time it takes to get a team of EMTs to the patients, having SAR personnel as trained EMTs makes sense. The SAR personnel are already there and can start to work on the patient or patients.

People who have been lost for some time may have any of a variety of different medical conditions. Some may have broken bones or other injuries. Others may be dehydrated from lack of water, suffer from hypothermia or frostbite in cold areas, or have heat stress in hot climates. The SAR EMTs must work quickly to get the patients

Search and rescue (SAR) and Wilderness-EMT (W-EMT) first responders use whatever means are available to access patients in remote areas. Helicopters are an excellent means of transportation.

stabilized and ready to be rescued. Because this type of rescue is so specialized, there is a specific certification for SAR personnel called Wilderness EMT (W-EMT).

Wilderness EMT

Wilderness rescue teams have one of the most thrilling jobs of all first responders. They are on call twenty-four hours a day and can be woken up in the middle of the night to rescue an injured camper lost somewhere in a remote area. They travel to the scene, either by wilderness vehicle or helicopter, with a load of equipment, including emergency medicine gear, a supply of food and water, and personal safety gear. Once they arrive at the site, they might have to battle not only the darkness, but also the elements such as rain and cold temperatures, and wild animals.

The Wilderness EMT program teaches slightly different skills than the regular EMT programs. Regular EMTs are usually concerned with stabilizing patients, preparing them for transport, and then moving them to a hospital where doctors take over the medical care. A W-EMT does not usually have the option of immediate transport to a hospital. As a result, W-EMTs are trained in extended patient management. This means that W-EMTs must know how to administer IV fluids and give medications. They must also be trained in how to monitor patients and respond immediately to any medical conditions that develop.

Because wilderness rescue is often carried out in less-than-ideal conditions for treating patients, W-EMTs must be aware of and able to deal with shock, hypothermia, or heat stress. They must do all this while taking

Rescuing people from swift water is dangerous for everyone involved. The skills of water rescue first responders can be the difference between life and death for both the patient and the rescuer.

care of themselves in addition to the patient. W-EMTs also work in isolated settings, which are often far from hospitals. Because of this isolation, W-EMTs often have limited medical supplies because they must carry every-thing they use.

Water Rescue

Some first responders receive specialized training in performing water rescues. When heavy storms dump lots of rain, a dam breaks, or very heavy snows melt, rivers can overflow. Water rescue specialists risk their lives to battle the rushing waters and perform daring life-saving maneuvers. Sometimes, the rescuers themselves are swept away and need to be rescued.

Like other rescue specialists, water rescuers often hold EMT certification. Additionally, they are usually trained in either swiftwater rescue or whitewater rescue. Swiftwater rescue is specialized training for professional rescue workers who need to understand water conditions and rescue techniques in fast-moving waters such as floodwaters. Whitewater rescue is specialized training given to people who work around extremely fast-moving water, such as river rafting guides and recreational boaters. Swiftwater and whitewater rescues are difficult because the fast water is dangerous to both the patient and the rescuer. Special techniques are often used to secure, reach, and rescue patients, often at great risk to the rescuers themselves.

When the rescuer has an EMT certification, it's good because medical help may be given immediately. Often, these types of rescues take place during storms, when it is difficult to get other EMTs with an ambulance to a site. The EMT at the scene can deal with the common medical problems such as restoring breathing and treating hypothermia or exposure. These EMTs often save lives due to their quick actions.

High-Angle Rescues

When a call comes in that someone is trapped on a cliff, first responders with special training are sent scrambling to answer the call. They use ropes and climbing equipment to quickly reach the stranded person. These rescues are dangerous because loose rocks may injure the rescuers or the patients. Also, the rescuers must know and understand how to safely use their equipment while reaching and treating the patient.

High-angle rescues, by definition, are performed whenever the slope of the ground is greater than a 60° angle. This usually means cliffs or very steep hillsides. Rescues from these places require that rescuers use ropes to reach patients. Two other classifications are also based on the slope of the ground. They are low angle (15° to 35°) and steep angle (36° to 60°). Low-angle and steep-angle rescues also require specialized rope techniques, but they are usually not as dangerous as high-angle rescues.

High-angle rescue first responders receive specialized training in rock climbing. These skills help the first responders to reach their patients and safely rescue them from this dangerous environment.

The patients in high-angle rescue are often rock climbers. They are frequently hurt as a result of a fall or by being hit by falling rocks. Many people trained in high-angle rescue are also EMT certified. As with other types of rescue situations, the rescuers must stabilize and treat the patient on the spot. What makes administering medical attention relatively difficult for the high-angle rescuer is that it is often done while the first responder is still attached to a rope and suspended far above the ground. However, many times, the injuries of the patient are critical and prompt action by the first responder is needed regardless of how difficult the rescue may be.

Once the patient is stabilized, he or she may be raised to the top of the angle, lowered to the bottom, or, in some extreme cases, lifted off the angle by a helicopter. These feats are often performed at great risk to the rescuers.

Cave Rescues

Sometimes accidents happen when people are exploring caves. These types of problems are particularly difficult for rescuers to deal with. The patient in a cave rescue is usually far from the entrance. A cave rescue may involve elements of search and rescue, swiftwater, and high-angle rescue in addition to moving rescuers and equipment through tight spaces and total darkness. The rescuers depend on their lights and equipment to get them to the patient. Many cave rescue personnel have EMT certification because it's usually a long time between reaching the patient and when the patient is brought out of the cave.

The EMTs who are part of cave rescue teams have the difficult task of working under less-than-ideal conditions. Like other wilderness rescues, they work in locations that are very remote and have limited access to medical equipment. They must often improvise and make do with what they have. The rescuers also face problems such as the patient having hypothermia, serious injury, or dehydration. Small, narrow cave passages, underground rivers, vertical drops, and total darkness often complicate these conditions.

People who work in specialized rescue fields such as search and rescue, high-angle rescue, and cave rescue have an exceptionally difficult job. In many cases, these people are the first on the scene in remote areas, just like police, firefighters, and paramedics. It may take considerable time for EMTs to reach such patients, and the patients must be stabilized before the EMTs arrive. This often has to be done in the harshest of conditions.

First responders who have unique skills use them in ways that are much different than those responding to a routine accident in an ambulance within an urban area. First response services operate more efficiently in urban settings because hospitals are usually close to the patient and emergency response times are short. In harsh wilderness environments, however, first responders have a much harder time rescuing patients. This is the reason why there is a growing need for specialized rescue personnel, such as Wilderness EMTs and cave rescuers, among others.

First Response Today

In 2006, the population of the United States reached 300 million. A large percentage of these people live in urban areas. Because much of the population is concentrated in these developed areas, providing first response is simplified. However, because of the growing population, we are around more chemicals that can harm us. These hazardous materials pose a risk to first responders when they perform their jobs.

Hazardous Materials

Hazardous materials (HazMat) surround us all every day. The fuel in our vehicles, cleaners under the kitchen sink, paints, and solvents, among other things, are all around us. Most do not pose much risk

First responders may need to enter areas where hazardous chemicals have been spilled, such as in accidents involving tanker trucks.

because we use them in small quantities. However, these same chemicals in large quantities can be quite dangerous.

Almost all first responders have some form of training in dealing with HazMats. HazMat training gives first responders the knowledge they need to assess a potentially hazardous situation. For example, if first responders report to an accident and, as part of that accident, a tanker truck has spilled its load, they know how to respond to the spill. The first responders would try to determine what the material is and then be able to tell whether they needed to wear protective suits and have self-contained air sources, or if they could enter the scene of the accident without protective gear.

HazMat training also includes learning how to decontaminate patients. When a patient is exposed to hazardous materials, the contaminants need to be removed as soon as possible. Different chemicals have different decontamination requirements. Some may be as simple as washing them off with soap and water while others may involve using other chemicals to neutralize the substance. These procedures require specialized training so that first responders perform the job without harming themselves or others.

Having knowledge of HazMats also helps first responders deal with patients who have been exposed to hazardous substances themselves. This knowledge of hazardous materials helps first responders determine the best course of action to preserve the patient's safety. As you can see, HazMat training helps first responders work effectively under all conditions involving dangerous chemicals.

Natural Disasters

HazMat training also helps first responders when they must deal with natural disasters. Natural disasters include earthquakes, hurricanes, volcanic eruptions, tornadoes, and floods. These disasters damage buildings and roads. That damage, in turn, can cause injury to people. When a natural disaster strikes a large urban area, first responders are called on to provide emergency care for the many who are affected.

Having to care for many patients, of course, is more complicated than dealing with one or two patients at a time. One way first responders deal with large numbers of injured people is to set up aid stations where patients can first be brought. First responders work to bring patients to an aid station. There, the extent of their injuries is assessed. The assessment of patients determines the order in which they are transferred to a hospital for more care. This process is called triage. Triage is a system used by emergency personnel to ration medical resources when the number of injured people needing care exceeds the resources available.

These spray-painted directions were used after the September
11, 2001, terrorist attacks. There were so many patients that
a triage system was established.

Triage helps first responders treat the greatest number of
patients possible in these dire situations.

When a patient is triaged, he or she is assessed and a
determination is made about what should be done to
treat him or her. A patient with minor injuries may be set
aside, while more critical ones are given care. A critical
patient may be sent immediately to a hospital for surgery.
Some patients whose injuries are so bad that they will
likely not survive may simply be looked after. This frees

up lifesaving medical resources for patients more likely to survive. Triage may sound cruel, but during a natural disaster, the number of patients will likely far exceed the resources that doctors and hospitals can supply.

Terrorism

Like natural disasters, terrorist attacks can severely stress first responder capabilities. A terrorist attack may injure or kill tens, hundreds, or even thousands of people. The terrorist attack on the World Trade Center on September 11, 2001, created chaos for emergency services in New York City. The collapse of the World Trade Center towers killed 479 first responders, many of them firefighters. These first responders entered the building to bring out as many people as they could. Many lives were saved because of their efforts.

Response to a terrorist attack presents many problems for first responders. First, the sheer number of patients with injuries may be overwhelming. Second, access to outside medical help may be disrupted, so a triage system would have to be implemented. Third, the first responders and patients may be exposed to hazardous

chemicals or conditions. Finally, there may be long-term health effects from being exposed to such hazards.

As with any disaster, the risk of exposure to hazardous materials in a terrorist attack is great. It is possible that a terrorist attack may include some type of biological, chemical, or nuclear weapon. These can include

First responders are often among the first on the scene of terrorist attacks. Being the first to respond to the September 11 attacks in New York, many rescuers perished.

biological agents such as anthrax or smallpox, chemical agents such as nerve gas, or nuclear agents such as radioactive materials.

Since September 11, 2001, first responders have started undergoing specialized training to respond to terrorist attacks. It is difficult to predict the type of attack terrorists might enact or the scenario in which it will take place, which is why training for all possibilities is so important.

The Future of First Responders

Emergency medical services is still an expanding field, and it will likely continue to grow. As the population increases, the chance of accidents requiring first responders also increases. Additionally, as the population continues to age, the demand for EMTs and paramedics will grow. The elderly often have more health issues and require more ambulance trips to the hospital than younger people. Part of the task of dealing with the elderly will be taken up by an increase in private ambulance services. These services will also hire many EMTs to staff their ambulances.

In addition to new jobs being created, there is also a high turnover rate among EMTs. Some EMTs leave the field to take related positions, while others leave to enter medical programs to become registered nurses or doctors. Some move on because of the stressful working conditions. Others go on to pursue related careers in first response.

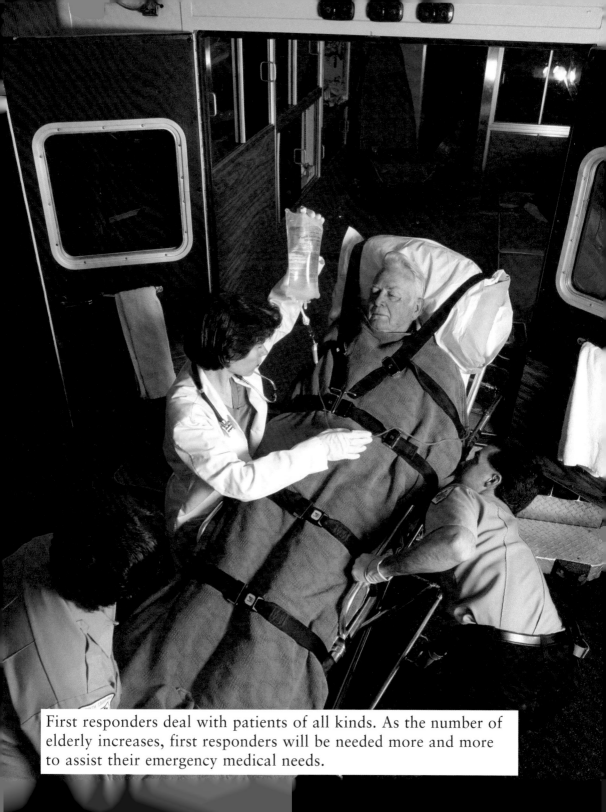

First responders deal with patients of all kinds. As the number of elderly increases, first responders will be needed more and more to assist their emergency medical needs.

Today, first responders have a much different job than emergency professionals ever had before. In the past, much of the U.S. population lived outside of cities, and emergency health care was minimal at best. Today, the population has shifted to urban areas, so people are more concentrated. First responders operate efficiently in these types of settings because hospitals are usually close to the patient and response times are shorter. The need for specialized rescue personnel continues, but as the population changes, the nature of the first responder's job also changes.

Glossary

AIDS (acquired immunodeficiency syndrome) This blood-borne virus is marked by a breakdown of the body's immune system.

anatomy The study of the structure of the human body.

cardiac Relating to the heart.

CPR (cardiopulmonary resuscitation) An emergency procedure, often employed after cardiac arrest in which cardiac massage, artificial respiration, and drugs are used to maintain the circulation of oxygenated blood to the brain.

defibrillator An electrical device used to counteract an unusual rhythm of the heart muscle and restore normal heartbeat by applying a brief electric shock.

EKG (electrocardiogram) An instrument used in the detection and diagnosis of heart abnormalities. It measures electrical activity on the body's surface and generates a record of the electrical currents associated with heart muscle activity.

esophageal Relating to the esophagus, which is the tube that transports food, water, and oxygen into the body.

extracurricular Work experience that is performed outside of normal school schedules.

frostbite Injury or destruction of skin and underlying tissue resulting from prolonged exposure to freezing or subfreezing temperatures.

gurney A metal stretcher with wheeled legs used for transporting patients.

heat stress A heat-related ailment such as heatstroke or heat exhaustion.

hepatitis A contagious disease characterized by an inflammation of the liver.

hypothermia Abnormally low body temperature.

intravenous (IV) A method for transporting fluids to a patient through his or her veins.

paramedic A person who is trained to give emergency medical treatment or assist medical professionals.

physiology The biological study of the functions of living organisms and their parts.

shock A potentially fatal physiological reaction to a variety of conditions, including illness, injury, hemorrhage, and dehydration, usually characterized by loss of blood pressure, diminished blood circulation, and inadequate blood flow to the tissues.

trauma A serious injury or shock to the body, as from an accident.

triage A system used by emergency medical personnel to ration limited medical resources when the number of injured needing care exceeds the resources available. This allows emergency medical personnel to treat the greatest number of patients possible.

For More Information

Department of Homeland Security
Washington, D.C. 20528
(202) 282-8000
Web site: http://www.dhs.gov

Federal Emergency Management Agency (FEMA)
Office of the Director
500 C Street SW
Washington, D.C. 20472
(800) 621-FEMA (3362)
Web site: http://www.fema.gov

First Responder, Inc.
12816 Shelly Lane
Plainfield, IL 60544
(815) 577-6437

Web site: http://www.frinc.net
E-mail: info@frinc.net

First Responder Institute
15312 Spencerville Court, Suite 100
Burtonsville, MD 20866
(301) 421-0096
Web site: http://www.firstresponder.org

National Association of Emergency Medical Technicians
P.O. Box 1400
Clinton, MS 39060-1400
(800) 34-NAEMT (346-2368)
Web site: http://www.naemt.org
E-mail: info@naemt.org

National Association of EMS Educators
Foster Plaza 6
681 Andersen Drive
Pittsburgh, PA 15220
(412) 920-4775
Web site: http://www.naemse.org
E-mail: naemse@naemse.org

National Association of EMS Physicians
P.O. Box 15945-281
Lenexa, KS 66285-5945
(800) 228-3677
Web site: http://www.naemsp.org
E-mail: info-naemsp@goAMP.com

Web Sites

Due to the changing nature of Internet links, the Rosen Publishing Group, Inc., has developed an online list of Web sites related to the subject of this book. This site is updated regularly. Please use this link to access the list:

http://www.rosenlinks.com/ec/first

For Further Reading

Bowman-Kruhm, Mary. *The Kids' Career Library: A Day in the Life of an Emergency Medical Technician (EMT)*. New York, NY: The Rosen Publishing Group, Inc., 1997.

Bryan, Nichol. *Paramedics* (Everyday Heroes). New York, NY: Checkerboard Books, 2002.

Ferry, Monica. *Search-and-Rescue Specialist and Careers in FEMA* (Homeland Security and Counterterrorism Careers). Berkeley Heights, NJ: Enslow Publishers, 2006.

Gibson, Karen Bush. *Emergency Medical Technicians*. Mankato, MN: Bridgestone Books, 2001.

Kalman, Bobbie. *Emergency Workers Are on Their Way!* (My Community and Its Helpers). New York, NY: Crabtree Publishing, 2002.

Peltak, Jennifer. *Call to Rescue, Call to Heal: Emergency Medical Professionals at Ground Zero (United We Stand)*. New York, NY: Chelsea House Publishers, 2002.

Primm, Russel. *Emergency Medical Technician (Careers Without College)*. Mankato, MN: Capstone Press, 1998.

Thompson, Tamara. *Emergency Response* (Careers for the Twenty-First Century). San Diego, CA: Lucent Books, 2004.

Bibliography

Cooper, Donald C. *Fundamentals of Search and Rescue.* Boston, MA: Jones & Bartlett Publishers, 2005.

Karam, J. A. *Into the Breach: A Year of Life and Death with EMS.* New York, NY: St. Martin's Press, 2002.

Haskell, Guy. *Emergency Medical Technician-Intermediate: Pearls of Wisdom* (Pearls of Wisdom). Boston, MA: Boston Medical Publishing, 1999.

Larmon, Baxter. *Basic Life Support Skills.* Upper Saddle River, NJ: Prentice Hall, 2004.

Lipke, Rick. *Technical Rescue Riggers Guide.* Bellingham, WA: Conterra, Inc., 1997.

Mistovich, Joseph. *Prehospital Emergency Care Workbook.* Upper Saddle River, NJ: Prentice Hall, 2003.

Pendley, Tom. *Technical Rescue Field Operations Guide.* Glendale, AZ: Desert Rescue Research, 1999.

Index

About the Author

Allan B. Cobb is a writer and editor living in central Texas. When he isn't writing and editing, he spends as much time as possible outdoors. He enjoys hiking, backpacking, canoeing, kayaking, and camping. He also enjoys exploring caves. His travels have taken him all around the world, and he is trained in first aid and CPR. He has also had additional training in cave rescue techniques and has participated in a number of cave rescues.

Photo Credits

Cover © David J. Philip/AP/Wide World Photos, p. 6 © Ariel Skelley/Corbis; p. 8 Robyn Beck/AFP/Getty Images; p. 11 © Lisette Le Bon/SuperStock; p. 14 © Mike Wintroath/AP/Wide World Photos; p. 17 © AP Photo/The Plain Dealer; p. 19 Laurence Gough/iStock International, Inc.; p. 22 © Eric Reed/AP/Wide World Photos; p. 25 © Nati Harnik/AP/Wide World Photos; p. 27 courtesy of Rescue Training, Inc.; p. 28 © LM Otero/AP/Wide World Photos; p. 32 © Keith Johnson/ksl Chopper 5/AP/Wide World Photos; pp. 34–35 © Brian Nicholson/AP/Wide World Photos; p. 38 © Ed Kashi/Corbis; p. 43 Mark Wilson/Getty Images; p. 46 © Beth A. Keiser/AP/Wide World Photos; pp. 48–49 © Neville Elder/Corbis; p. 51 © Will & Deni McIntyre/Photo Researchers, Inc.

Editor: Nicholas Croce; Photo Researcher: Hillary Arnold